STARGAZERS

PHIL CARRADICE

Published by Accent Press Ltd 2017

ISBN 9781786152961

The Quick Reads project in Wales is an initiative coordinated by the Welsh Books Council and supported by the Welsh Government.

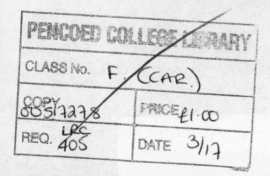

Chapter One

The early sunlight glinted like shards of silver off Yaniv's armour. A short stabbing sword with its elegant ebony grip, given to all Palace Guards on enlistment, hung lightly at his side. He held it to his thigh as his horse plodded easily forwards among the twelve-strong troop, and smiled happily.

Then, an unexpected doubt eased into his mind. Would he, Yaniv wondered, be ready when the moment came? Would he be able to cope in the cut and thrust of battle, would he ever be good enough?

He shook his head to clear away the thoughts and glanced across at the man riding alongside him - Omar, the veteran of a dozen campaigns, victor and vanquished in hundreds of desert battles.

Yaniv envied the old soldier his confidence, his easy way of riding, even the scar across his left cheek. He doubted he would ever be so sure of himself.

As he watched the old man from the corner of his eye, Omar looked up, winked

1

and grinned at him.

'Cheer up, lad,' he drawled. 'We'll soon be rid of this lot.'

He pointed at Yaniv's gleaming breastplate and the tall plumed helmet that all Guards wore. Yaniv stared at him, not understanding.

'All this useless junk,' Omar said. 'Another hour and we'll be well away from the city. Then we can dump the gear in one of the wagons and ride like proper fighting men. After all, it's only for show, so the people can see us in all our glory.'

He paused and stretched in the saddle, squinting at the low sun that was still climbing over the western hills.

'Not that there were many of them to watch us leave this morning. A God-forsaken time to start any patrol, I say.'

Yaniv nodded, pulling at his body armour where it had ridden up and was now digging into his neck. Omar studied him.

'You'll be all right, boy,' he said at last.

'Really? How can you tell?'

Omar shrugged and eased his weight back in the saddle.

'I just know. Call it a gut feeling. Of course, nobody can really know, not one hundred percent. If we did there'd be a hell of a lot less grief around the place, I can tell you, and fewer snotty-nosed officers thinking they can change the world in a moment. No, nobody knows how they're going to react until they see the first flight of arrows blotting out the sun. But when you've been around as long as I have, you get a feeling about people, good or bad. And I tell you, you'll be all right.'

Yaniv set his gaze on the far hills. He thought about the old soldier's words. They were reassuring but, at the end of the day, they were still only words. If only he could be as sure as Omar. His mind began to wander back over the events of the past few days. So much had happened.

* * *

Right from the beginning, Yaniv's mother had been against it.

'He's only sixteen, for God's sake,' she had stormed.

Nearly seventeen, Yaniv thought but, wisely, kept silent. Miriam Sharon was standing in the courtyard of their house, a cool, quiet spot, surrounded by high walls and lemon and olive trees to give shade.

The house stood on a small rise half a mile beyond the city wall where the cool summer breeze and the welcome winter sun were regular visitors. The soft red sandstone of the city buildings shimmered distantly and,

3

despite his mother's anger and temper, Yaniv was glad to be away from the stench of unwashed bodies and rotting rubbish that always seemed to hang around the place. He had seen the gangs of prisoners whose job it was to keep the city clean, sullen and unhappy men who went about their job in a half-hearted and resentful way. He was sure there must be a better system than using what was little more than slave labour.

'It's not right!' his mother shouted, bringing him back to the present. 'He's too young.'

Yaniv's father, Daniel Sharon, was sprawled across a wooden bench set against the rear wall of the house. A Sergeant in the Palace Guard, Daniel was a tall, tough man, confident in his rank and ability.

'I was twelve when I fought my first action,' he shrugged. 'The boy's got four years on me.'

Miriam stamped her foot. 'Don't be ridiculous, Daniel. You were always meant to be a soldier. I thought Yaniv might be a doctor or a physician. Or maybe a lawgiver. That was my dream for him.'

'Your dream, Miriam, not mine. And not Yaniv's either, eh boy?'

Daniel and Miriam stared at Yaniv. He was leaning against a shadowing mulberry tree, already dressed in his new leather tunic and

4

leggings. He nodded in agreement with his father's words.

'See, Miriam?' said Daniel. 'The world will always want soldiers. And Yaniv wants to be one.' His eyes twinkled. 'Besides, I didn't hear you complain when we started courting. You knew what my job was.'

Miriam snorted and glared at him. 'The world's more civilised now. At least that's one thing the Romans brought, a little peace, with no need for boys to go marching off to war.'

Yaniv stepped forward, unable to stay silent any longer.

'It's not war, Mother, just a short patrol, taking people over the mountains. And whatever you say, I really do want to go.'

Daniel grinned contentedly and spread his arms.

'See? The boy's right. This job will mean just a few weeks away, a gentle ride across the desert and then up over the mountains. All we're doing is providing a guard for two of the Palace stargazers.'

Miriam snarled. She snatched a lemon from the tree and hurled it at her husband. The fruit smashed into the wall beside his head. Daniel stared at the mess, then back at his wife.

'Not quite ripe yet, my love.'

Yaniv tried hard not to grin – his mother's

5

tempers were famous but Daniel seemed to have a way of dealing with them.

'Stargazers?' Miriam shouted. 'What do they want to go travelling out of the kingdom for? They've got it made, lying in luxury up there at the Palace, staring at the Heavens day and night.'

Yaniv sighed. He supposed there was more to being a stargazer than just looking at the sky but, like Miriam, he did wonder what this trip was all about.

Daniel Sharon pulled himself to his feet and stared, forcefully, at his wife.

'It doesn't matter what they're going to do. We don't need to know. We're just soldiers, there to protect them. That's all we need to worry about.' He laid his hand on Miriam's arm. 'You can complain all you like but the deed is done. The boy is enlisted in the Palace Guard. He starts his formal training the day we get back and whatever he learns on this trip will put him well ahead of the other new recruits at the Academy.'

Miriam shook her arm free and would have said more but, at that moment, a servant appeared to tell them that the midday meal was ready. They went into the dark coolness of the house, Miriam still seething and angry.

It was one of the benefits of Daniel Sharon's

job, this house, gifted to him by the Palace for as long as he served. And Daniel had no intention of ever stepping down or retiring. The rank of Sergeant in the Palace Guard gave him position and status in the city.

The argument went on, Miriam growing more heated by the minute. Despite Daniel's attempts to keep her calm, her temper finally boiled over. She slammed down her knife and the delicate terracotta dish in front of her shattered. Hurling back her stool, she stormed off to her room.

'She'll come round, boy,' Daniel smiled. 'Don't worry about it. She just needs time and a bit of space - both of which she'll get tomorrow, after we've gone. Don't worry.'

Yaniv did not worry. He and his father had signed the enlistment papers, he had his uniform and tomorrow morning he would set out on his first patrol. His mother could protest all she liked but it was already far too late.

* * *

'Did your parents mind you becoming a soldier?' Yaniv asked Omar as they rode on across the flat plain. 'I mean, did they object?'

The old soldier shrugged. 'That was so long ago, it's hard to remember. I don't think they objected. It was what I wanted to do and, to be honest, it meant one less mouth to feed back home.' He paused and glanced at Yaniv. 'It wouldn't be Sergeant Sharon, so I guess your mother has had a few concerns about you joining the Guard. Am I right?'

Yaniv nodded glumly. 'She wouldn't listen to anything I said. Or to Father, either. Even when I told her about the places I'd see or go to as a soldier. She wasn't interested. I bet you've seen lots of places, lots of different countries, Omar.'

A satisfied gleam of happiness began to spread across the old man's face. He sat back on his saddle, eyes far away and dreaming.

'A few, not as many as some, more than others. Palestine, Jordan, Egypt – now Egypt, that's the place, a land of milk and honey, as they say. All those temples and the River Nile, a wonderful place, boy, wonderful.'

They rode on as the old man spoke and the sun rose higher in the sky.

Chapter Two

That first day, riding across the desert with the troop, Yaniv felt as if he did nothing but talk and listen. Daniel Sharon had chosen Yaniv's riding partner well. The old soldier was a mine of information. All morning he pointed out landmarks and passed on valuable tips to the young man.

'Where's your oilskin?' Omar asked as they all stopped, just before noon, to rest the horses.

Yaniv looked blank. Omar shook his head.

'I can see Sergeant Sharon really is letting you learn on the job. Here, I have a spare one you can use. Make sure you buy one when we get back to the city.'

He passed across a length of heavy black material. Without this, he explained, Yaniv's blankets would be soaking within an hour when they came to bed down for the night.

'More valuable to a soldier than a sword or spear,' he said, showing Yaniv how to use the oilskin. 'Look. You just fold it in two and get inside - one piece of oilskin below you, the other above. Protects you and your blankets from the dew or the rain.'

The troop remounted and they rode steadily on. Towards mid-afternoon orders came down the column for Omar to ride ahead and scout out the terrain. With a nod and a wink to Yaniv, he galloped off, leaving the young man to think back over the events of a fascinating day.

* * *

Yaniv and his father had left home early in the morning, just before first light. To begin with, his mother had been still angry. Only at the final moment did she begin to soften.

'Remember,' she said at last, 'if you get killed don't you come back here and complain to me.'

'No, Mother,' Yaniv grinned.

'Very well,' Miriam tutted, pushing her hair into place, 'get along with you. Both of you get along.'

They walked through still and empty streets, then cut through the Medina towards the Palace gates. Daniel stopped, suddenly, and turned to face his son.

'Remember, Yanni, you'll get no favours from me on this trip. It's not like one of our hunting expeditions. This is real soldiering and from now on, you're just one of the troop.

10

We're not related.'

Yaniv nodded and followed his father along the lanes. Huddled shapes lay against the walls or in the doorways. Yaniv stared at the bundles of human misery and squalor and for the twentieth time that morning blessed his own good fortune. There was so much poverty here in the city and no-one seemed willing to do anything about it.

They passed into the Palace grounds through a small door in the main gate. The other members of the troop, all eleven of them, were waiting in the courtyard, some sitting on the ground, others slouched against the wall. One or two were making last minute adjustments to their saddles or heaving heavy goods into the backs of the waiting wagons.

'All present and correct, sir.'

A short dark man sidled up to Daniel Sharon. He had ferret eyes and a faint smell of sweat came from his armpits. As he pulled himself erect to salute the Sergeant, Yaniv could not help thinking there was a hint of sarcasm in the gesture.

'This is Corporal Tomas,' said Daniel, jerking his thumb towards his second-in-command. 'Tomas, this is my son, Yaniv Sharon.'

The Corporal grinned at Yaniv but the smile did not reach his eyes. Before he could say anything Daniel Sharon cut in.

'My son, yes, but he is to get no special treatment, understand? He's just a trooper like everyone else. No special treatment.'

Corporal Tomas shrugged and Yaniv saw dislike - of Daniel or anyone in a position of power - flash across his face.

'Right, sir, no special treatment - you can rely on me.'

There was a clatter of horses' hooves, loud as a kettledrum, and a huge green coach rolled through the archway that led to the inner part of the Palace. Travelling trunks and large canvas bags were strapped to its roof and it was pulled by four white horses. The vehicle, even to inexperienced eyes like Yaniv's, seemed dangerously overloaded.

'What in the name of God do we have here?' asked Daniel, staring at the coach.

'For the stargazers, sir,' shrugged Tomas.

Daniel shook his head in disbelief.

'How the hell do they expect to get that across the mountains?'

Tomas could hardly stop himself grinning at the Sergeant's discomfort. He jerked his thumb over his shoulder towards the elegant balconies and terraces of the Palace.

'Orders from above, sir.'

'God give me strength,' Daniel whispered as

he strode off to check the coach harnesses. Yaniv watched him go.

'All right, boy,' Tomas barked suddenly. 'You heard the Sergeant, no special treatment, no favours. Get your horse sorted out. Move it!'

Just before the fourth hour, the Palace doors swung open and three muffled figures glided down the steps. Without a glance at the soldiers, they climbed quickly into the waiting coach.

'Three?' asked Yaniv, turning to the old soldier who had been detailed as his riding partner. 'I thought it was supposed to be two.'

'Two, three, who knows?' Omar shrugged. 'They seem to have changed their minds and added another to the party. You'll notice that they don't give us any extra soldiers, mind you. That's too much to hope for. Three it is and ours not to reason why.'

Daniel Sharon gave the order to mount and the men heaved themselves into their saddles. They trotted easily down the track from the Palace, two outriders leading the way, followed by the stargazers' coach. The rest of the troop fell in behind. Lastly came two open wagons full of supplies and equipment.

Their road skirted the city boundary, the low red buildings already beginning to shimmer and seethe under the morning sun.

Slowly the convoy moved out onto the flat desert plain.

* * *

'Trooper Sharon!'

The Corporal's voice rasped like a carpenter's saw through the late afternoon heat, breaking into Yaniv's daydreams. He wheeled around at the sound, almost losing his balance and having to grab at the saddle pommel to keep his seat.

'My God!' sighed Tomas, reining in alongside him. 'What are they sending us now? Babies just out of their blankets?'

The soldiers within earshot laughed but there was nothing vindictive in the sound. Yaniv even managed to join in with the merriment.

'You'd best practise your riding skills, Trooper Sharon,' continued the Corporal. 'A cavalry man who can't ride is no use to anyone.' He pointed towards the tail end of the column. 'We'll start right now. Take the rear, Trooper Sharon, eat a little dirt for a while.'

Yaniv turned his horse and trotted to the back of the line. As he went, he heard the sneering bark of the little Corporal's final taunt.

'He'll get no favours from me. Just because

14

he's the Sergeant's son, he thinks he's entitled to special treatment. Well, he's wrong about that.'

Yaniv pushed down his anger. He had never asked for favours, never expected any. Already it was clear that if Tomas could not get to the Sergeant, he would enjoy taking his anger out on his son.

With evening approaching, Daniel Sharon wanted to make use of the light while it lasted. At his order, the troopers urged their horses into a canter, the two wagons bouncing along in their wake.

Their route lay across a wide stretch of desert tundra. The wasteland was dotted with palm trees and strange green plants with spikes as big as a man's forefinger. Ahead of the riders, like a long low cloud on the horizon, lay the mountain range they would have to cross and Daniel Sharon intended to reach the foot of those hills before night closed in.

Yaniv quickly discovered that the Corporal's comment about 'eating dirt' had been accurate. At the tail of the column, dust constantly found its way into his mouth and eyes. It even managed to squirm into his nostrils and no amount of blowing could clear it. The heat was stifling, like a baker's oven, as Yaniv turned his head from side to side in an attempt to avoid the worst of the dust.

For twenty minutes they rode, Yaniv with his head bowed and wishing for night to come. Just in front of him was one of the supply wagons, the last vehicle in the column. After a while, he noticed a tall girl, handsome rather than pretty, watching him from the back of the wagon. She was, he thought, about the same age as him but much more experienced. There was nothing superior about her but he guessed there was much he could learn from her. As if to prove the point, she suddenly spoke.

'Try putting your neckerchief across your mouth and nose. It's not there just for show, you know.'

He raised an arm in reply, wondering why he had never thought of such a simple solution. Tying the scarf across his face, he felt instantly better.

When, an hour later, his father called a halt, Yaniv dismounted and stood for a few minutes alongside the wagon. The girl's name was Sarah. She knew no other, her parents having died many years before. Growing up on the streets of the city, the luxury of a last name had been denied her.

'Sarah's good enough for me,' she declared.

She paused and stared at him from under

her fringe of jet-black hair.

'You're a bit young for a soldier, aren't you?'

Yaniv shrugged. 'It's my first job, guarding the stargazers on their journey. God knows where we're going or why. My father says it doesn't concern us.'

'Your father?'

'He's the Sergeant in charge of the troop.'

Sarah looked at him with renewed interest and respect.

'Sergeant Sharon, you're his son? He's one of the better ones. Most soldiers don't even know we exist - although they'd soon be shouting if their food and equipment suddenly went missing.' She smiled at Yaniv. 'Don't go getting your hopes up. We're part of the Palace Supply Team, which means we wash clothes and prepare food for people like your stargazers. Important people - which doesn't usually include soldiers, unless you're very lucky.'

She paused and pushed, coyly, at the desert sand with her sandal.

'Sergeant Sharon's boy, eh? I like him, he always asks after us, makes sure we've got what we need to do our job. He even gets us good quarters when we stop at a village inn. Yes, he's a good one - if you turn out to be half the man he is you'll be all right.'

She turned her head away and spat onto the sand.

'Not like that Corporal Tomas, him and his shifty little eyes. Always watching, that's him. I wouldn't trust him as far as a donkey can piss. He frightens me.'

Yaniv wondered, briefly, if this girl could ever be frightened of anything. Yet her tone had gone suddenly cold and Yaniv guessed there had been bad blood between her and Corporal Tomas in the past. For a moment, Sarah glared at him, her gaze seeming to say that all men were worthless and not to be trusted. Then she shook her head.

'Sorry, Yaniv, it's not you, it's just that little weasel.'

'Have you done lots of trips like this?' Yaniv asked, trying hard to lighten the mood.

'More than a few,' said the girl, beginning to relax again. 'All part of the job – mind you, this bit is easy, just dirt and dust. You wait until we get up into the mountains. Then you'll really start to earn your pay, soldier boy.'

'Thanks,' Yaniv grinned. 'As if this hasn't been bad enough.'

'Trooper Sharon!'

The shrill voice of Corporal Tomas cut through the air like a whistle.

'My master calls,' Yaniv quipped.

18

The girl smiled at him. 'Go and play at soldiers, Yanni. Maybe I'll see you later.'

'I hope so,' he said as he pulled himself into his saddle and rode back down the length of the column.

* * *

They camped that night alongside a river that came tumbling down from the hills. Ahead of them were the first folds of the mountain range. From a distance they had seemed low and gentle but now, close up, they reared like a massive fist into the night sky.

The stargazers' coach was pulled into a grove of lemon trees. As soon as the wheels stopped rolling, the Palace servants surrounded it with a high wicker screen.

'Fair enough,' Yaniv shrugged, 'I suppose they want their privacy.'

Omar hawked up a mouthful of phlegm and spat it onto the ground.

'If they don't want to be seen that's their business. We'll be comfortable enough – nothing like a good fire after a day's ride, boy.'

They set a guard, gathered kindling, then lit their fires on the riverbank. The light of the flames was bright against the darkness, twisting and coiling like golden dancing girls. Yaniv felt warmth and comfort surging through his bones. He smiled to himself. He had finished his first shift as a Palace Guard – his back and thighs might ache from the day's riding but nothing could take away his pride and the warm glow of companionship. He was starting to doze when Sarah ghosted up beside him.

'For you,' she said, holding out a pottery dish.

Yaniv took the dish and pulled back the covering cloth. Three steaming pastries, coated in sugar and filled with almonds and sultanas, lay before him.

'Left over from the stargazers' dinner,' the girl said. 'They'll never miss them.'

Then she was gone, back into the darkness beyond the fire's glow. Yaniv felt an elbow in his ribs.

'What it is to have friends in high places,' Omar grinned.

Yaniv broke up the pastries and shared them among the troop. Even Corporal Tomas, he noticed, came to take his share.

'I knew it was lucky to have the Sergeant's boy with us,' Omar said, glancing archly at the little Corporal.

Tomas did not respond. Yaniv rolled himself into his blanket and prepared to sleep.

'Boots?' Omar asked.

Yaniv pointed to the high cavalry boots

standing side by side on the sand beside his bedroll. Omar shook his head.

'Inside the blanket, boy. Important things, boots. Left out there anyone could help himself – or something unpleasant could crawl inside. Cuddle up to them, Yanni, keep them warm in the night.'

Yaniv tucked his boots into his blanket and lay back. He dozed, half listening to the call of the cicadas and the low rumble of conversation from those soldiers still awake. He would not have wanted to be anywhere else in the whole wide world.

Towards midnight, Sergeant Sharon appeared amongst them. He laughed and joked with the men, squatting on the ground beside the fire. With a glow of satisfaction, Yaniv realised that his father was as popular with the troopers as he was with Sarah and the servants.

'Tomorrow's route,' Daniel said, suddenly. 'Straight up and keep going till the top. Then we go down the other side.'

'Whose bright idea was that?' asked Corporal Tomas. 'Don't tell me, our wonderful stargazers. You know what the terrain is like up there, sir, rocks and more bloody rocks. If you ask me it's nothing short of stupid.'

Daniel Sharon glared at him.

'But you see, Corporal,' he sneered, 'nobody did ask you. The stargazers chose the route and our destination. We don't have to worry about it – we just keep them safe.'

There was a rumble of agreement from the soldiers.

'We'll get them over the mountain, Sergeant,' one declared. 'Personally I'd prefer to push the buggers – all that Palace lot – off the top but duty is duty. We'll get them there, wherever "there" might be.'

Daniel Sharon grinned at the speaker.

'I see your politics haven't changed since the last time we rode together, Trooper Hussain.'

Everyone laughed, Hussain more than anyone. Daniel Sharon hauled himself to his feet.

'A long day tomorrow,' he threw over his shoulder. 'Get your rest while you can.'

Later, after two hours of guard duty – the middle watch, thanks to Corporal Tomas, the most uncomfortable of all shifts – Yaniv settled down to grab a few more hours' rest. He stared up at the stars. They all seemed bright but one, in particular, sparkled and shone like gold.

'The Romans call it Venus,' said Omar from deep inside his blankets. 'Named after their goddess of love. Forget watching the stars,

Yanni, leave that to the stargazers. Get to sleep or you'll be good for nothing in the morning.'

The old soldier rolled onto his side and was asleep again in a moment.

Venus? wondered Yaniv. Maybe. Yet he had seen Venus before and it had never burned as brightly as this. The star or planet, or whatever it was, seemed to pulse and radiate with light.

Perhaps he would find the courage to approach the stargazers and ask them about it. Remote and distant as they were, surely they would be pleased to see him taking an interest in astronomy?

Before he could make a decision, Yaniv fell soundly asleep.

Chapter Three

Yaniv was woken next morning by a pattering of rain on his face. Grey clouds were racing in from above the mountains and there was a sharp bite to the wind.

'Come on,' said Omar. 'Get your gear stowed while it's still dry. Nobody needs wet bedding.'

Yaniv groaned and buried himself deeper into his blanket. Omar pushed him with his foot.

'Move, boy, this will be a deluge inside the hour.'

The old soldier was right. By the time they had snatched a hurried breakfast and broken camp, the rain was cascading down like a waterfall.

Yaniv sat in his saddle, shoulders hunched and head buried in his cape, as the stargazers' green coach rumbled past. He saw shapes moving inside and envied them their comfort. Who were these people, he wondered. Stargazers, yes, but what did that really mean? And what on earth were they after on this trip? He would have dearly loved to know.

All morning they battled against the elements, rain constantly smashing into their faces. At midday, they left the desert behind and began to pick their way across a carpet of small stones and boulders.

'Scree and debris from the mountain,' Omar said. 'Washed down by the rain and no good for horses' hooves – so go easy, boy.'

The track was wide but no matter how often they snaked from side to side, it was still steep. The stargazers' coach made slow progress, the horses straining at their harnesses. On several of the steepest sections, Daniel Sharon ordered support lines to be rigged, to keep the vehicle from sliding off the track. It was tough work and Yaniv was pleased when he and Omar were detailed to ride ahead of the column, clearing the largest stones from the path.

At last, they reached the end of the scree and began to climb the true flank of the mountain. The going was easier but the rain still fell and now the temperature began to drop. Horses slipped and stumbled on the glassy pathway and it took all of Yaniv's skill just to stay upright in the saddle.

'Hard going, Yanni,' grunted Omar. 'A good way to blood you, I'm thinking.'

'Maybe,' Yaniv retorted. 'I just know I've

never been so wet in my life.'

He ran a finger around his collar and a curtain of rain flowed down his neck onto his chest. Cursing, he shrugged himself deeper into his cape.

'I see you've picked up soldiers' language quickly enough,' Omar laughed. 'Your education is coming on apace.'

At the lunch break, taken where they stood alongside their horses, Yaniv saw Sarah plodding through the rain towards him. She was soaked to the skin, without the luxury of a soldier's cape to keep her warm and at least partially dry. A piece of coarse sacking across the shoulders was the best she could do for protection.

'Yanni,' she said, 'do you think I could talk with your father?'

Yaniv glanced across at Omar. The old soldier shrugged and Yaniv turned back to the girl.

'I don't see why not. I'll take you to him.'

The Sergeant was leaning against the back of the stargazers' coach, rain streaming down his face as he spoke to Corporal Tomas. Yaniv and Sarah came to a halt a few paces away.

'Sir? Could we have a word?'

Corporal Tomas spun around, eyes blazing in fury. Like everyone else, he was soaked and not enjoying the experience.

'Too wet for you, Trooper? You heard what the Sergeant said yesterday, no special treatment. Get back to your horse.'

Yaniv shook his head. 'It's not me, Corporal, it's Sarah. She's the one who wants to speak with the Sergeant.'

Tomas snarled but Daniel Sharon raised a hand before he had time to speak.

'Go on, girl, what is it?'

Sarah pushed back her soaking hair and turned to face the Sergeant.

'It's about tonight, sir. This rain won't stop, not for hours yet. But there's a cave, three or four miles ahead. I reckon two hours' ride up the mountain in this weather. It should keep us warm and dry through the night. It's big, sir, big enough to take the coach, the horses and us.'

'You know this cave?' Daniel Sharon said. 'You can get us there?'

'I think so,' Sarah nodded. 'My friends and I have used it many times. If you were to send Yaniv and me ahead, we could get fires lit for you and the stargazers.'

Tomas snorted and reached out for the girl's shoulder. He spun her around and pushed her away.

'Get back to your place, girl. We're soldiers –

27

we don't mind a little rain.'

Yaniv held on to his anger, knowing he should not react. But he really did not like this small, aggressive man and knew he was just seconds away from launching himself at his throat. Before he could do anything, his father spoke again.

'We might be soldiers, Corporal, but we're not stupid ones. If we spend the night out in weather like this, half the troop will be down with fever before breakfast - not to mention what it will do to the horses.'

He turned to Sarah. 'Take one of the pack horses. You can ride, I take it? Find me this cave. Yaniv, go with her.'

Yaniv and Sarah turned away, Sergeant Sharon's final words on the matter echoing across the mountain.

'Don't fail us, girl. I have a feeling that much depends on you finding us shelter for the night.'

* * *

'Do you really know where this cave is?' asked Yaniv.

They had been riding for an hour, climbing steadily over flat slabs of rock. Already the column was far behind, lost in a covering shroud of mist and rain. Sarah shrugged.

'Sort of - I'll recognise it when I see it. But

this light – it's so dark we could miss it in the gloom.'

'That,' said Yaniv, 'doesn't fill me with confidence.'

Sarah did not reply. Her eyes were searching the cliffs and rock walls, trying hard to spot the opening to the cave. Bent against the rain, they rode on.

In the end, they found the place quite easily. A blacker slab of darkness on the cliff to their left suddenly reared up in front of them.

'There,' said Sarah, 'there it is.'

She urged her horse into a canter and pulled up in front of a wide gash in the rock.

'Wait here,' Yaniv said. 'I'll go in first. There might be all sorts of wild animals in there, taking shelter from the rain.'

'Not on your life, soldier boy,' Sarah said. 'What, me wait here and let you have all the fun – not to mention boasting about how you found the place. Oh no, we go in together.'

There was no arguing and together they inched inside the cave. The cavern was huge, eighty or ninety metres across, and it seemed to be empty.

'Perfect,' said Yaniv. 'Let's get a few fires going, and then I'll drop some markers out on the track.'

He bent down over a bush of rosemary that

was growing just inside the entrance.

'Wait!'

Sarah's voice was harsh. She pushed Yaniv back and grabbed a long stick from the cave floor.

'Watch.'

She leapt forward, screaming at the top of her voice. Once, twice, three times, she smashed down with the stick. Four snakes promptly shot out of the depths of the bush, hissing in anger. The largest one reared up, fangs bared.

'Vipers,' Yaniv breathed.

He reached for his sword but Sarah stopped him with a raised hand.

'Leave them. They're a lot more scared of us than we are of them.'

'Speak for yourself,' Yaniv said, letting his sword arm drop.

With a final spit of venom, the vipers slid out of the cave. Sarah grinned.

'Now we can make a fire. The snakes won't come back while we're here.'

When the column pulled to a halt in front of the cave, an hour had passed. Yaniv and Sarah had three fires blazing and the troopers looked at them longingly.

'Horses first,' Daniel Sharon called. 'See to the horses before you look to yourselves.'

He pointed to the far wall and called out to the driver of the stargazers' coach.

'Over there, against the wall. We'll get you a fire directly.'

It took the troopers less than thirty minutes to set up camp inside the cave. The stargazers sought refuge yet again behind their wicker screen and soon the pungent smell of wet clothes drying began to spread across the cave.

'Like washday in my house,' said Trooper Hussain.

He, like the others, had already stripped off his soaking tunic and breeches. Modesty had no place compared to the need to get dry.

'Well done, Yaniv,' said Sergeant Sharon as he passed his son.

The Sergeant had spent the time overseeing the arrangements for the stargazers and his soldiers. His hair and clothes were still soaking - he would dry off when everything was settled.

'Nothing to do with me, sir,' Yaniv said. 'Sarah found the place, I just rode with her.'

The Sergeant nodded. 'I know. I'll speak to her later. So, how are you enjoying your first patrol?'

'Fine. There's just such a lot to learn.'

'Listen to what Omar tells you. He's a good man - you'll pick up a lot from him. Believe me, if he hasn't seen or done it, then it hasn't happened.'

Yaniv could not help himself, knowing even as he spoke that he was talking out of turn.

'He should be Corporal, Father, not Tomas.'

Daniel glared at him.

'It's sir, not father. And when you know a bit more about soldiering, boy, I'll be happy to listen to your opinions. Until then keep your comments to yourself.'

Yaniv coloured as his father turned away. He had gone just a few metres when he paused and spoke back over his shoulder.

'But between you and me – as father and son – I agree. I offered the position to Omar but he didn't want to know. This is his last mission, he tells me, says he's going to retire to some farm in Palestine. I can't see him as a farmer but it's none of my business. As for Tomas, he's a good soldier, too. Give him a chance – you don't always have to be a good man to be a good soldier.'

They slept that night with full bellies and the warmth of the fires filling the cave. Yaniv lay alongside Omar, watching the patterns cast by the flames on the roof above his head. He soon realised that Omar, too, was wide-awake.

'I hear this is your last job,' Yaniv whispered

when he was sure that no-one else could hear.

Omar turned onto his side and propped himself up on his elbow.

'I wonder who you've been talking to,' he said. 'Yes, my last job. After this trip, I hand in my sword and shield. My son has –'

'A son, you've got a son?'

'Don't be so shocked, Yanni, even soldiers are entitled to a private life. Yes, I have a son, a couple of years older than you. He farms alongside the River Jordan, nothing much, just a few fields of crops and a handful of sheep and goats. But it makes him a living and it's where I'm going when this patrol is over.'

He paused and sighed. 'Can you imagine it? Me, becoming a farmer at my age. God knows how I'll cope.'

'I think,' said Yaniv, 'that you could do whatever you set your mind to do. But I'll miss you – you've been so good to me, almost like a father.'

Omar seemed about to reply but then changed his mind. Some things were clearly best left unsaid. He shook his head.

'Go to sleep, Yanni, you're on guard in a few hours.'

How can I sleep? Yaniv thought. Everything was too interesting.

* * *

33

They set off at dawn the next day. It was still raining but now it was just a fine drizzle and more bearable than the downpour of yesterday. Yaniv felt almost sorry to leave the cave. It had become something of a home and he marked it down, as Sarah had done, for use on future patrols.

All morning they climbed steadily. The drizzle turned into a thin wet sleet and with a sudden drop in temperature Yaniv thought it would turn to snow in the hours ahead. He was right. By noon, thick snow was falling and, within minutes, was lying like a white Persian carpet over the hills.

Finally, close to the summit, they came to a high pass where the land fell away in a sheer drop. It was impossible to see the bottom of the chasm. When Yaniv shouted into the vast emptiness, his voice echoed and roared back at him like a bull elephant.

'There's our way,' announced Daniel Sharon, pointing to a narrow track that skirted the chasm.

The track was in two sections, a narrow walkway on the upper level and, six metres lower, a wider path for horses and carts. In dry conditions the route would have been difficult. After the recent rain and snow, it looked lethal.

'Ideal spot for a bandit attack,' said Tomas. 'Once we start across we'll be helpless.'

He spat derisively into the cavern and watched the spittle float away into the depths. Yaniv could not help agreeing with him. His father clearly felt the same.

'I agree,' said Sharon. 'I'll check it out before we start to move. Trooper Hussain, come with me.'

He turned to Tomas.

'Nobody moves until I get back, understand?'

Without waiting for a reply, he dismounted and, with Hussain dogging his steps, strode to the beginning of the tracks. The two men clambered up onto the upper walkway and within seconds were lost to view in the swirling snow.

The rest of the troop eased themselves off their horses and stood stamping their feet in the cold mountain air. The breath from the horses billowed around them like steam from a pan of boiling water. Time passed slowly – five minutes, ten, then thirty.

'Anything could have gone wrong,' said one of the soldiers, suddenly. 'Maybe they've been ambushed by bandits.'

Yaniv shuddered at the words. Trooper Liman, he knew, was a fawning, two-faced creature who was sure to tell Tomas exactly what he wanted to hear. However, this time he could so easily be right. Nobody knew what waited beyond the chasm or down the hillside out of their view.

'I reckon they're both dead,' Liman said, almost gleefully. 'What do you reckon, Corporal?'

Tomas stroked his chin, pushing his tongue into his cheek as he tried to assess the problem.

'Maybe – but we haven't heard anything, no shouts or screams. Then again, mountains play tricks with sound. But it'll be dark soon. We need to move or we'll be stuck here all night.'

Omar pushed forward and glared at him.

'The Sergeant said to stay here. It would need a damned clever bandit to take Daniel Sharon down. He'll be all right. Let's just wait a bit longer.'

Liman sidled up alongside Tomas and spoke quietly into his ear. Tomas listened, nodded and then spun around to face the troop.

'Right, I've made my decision. Sharon is out of the picture. He may be dead, or he could be on his way back right now. We don't know.'

He looked directly at Yaniv.

'Either way, I'm now in charge. And I say we move off. We'll fix up a couple of landlines, tie them to the front and back of the coach – two of you can take the strain, from up there.'

He pointed to the footpath on top of the rock wall. Then his gaze moved to the path below.

'It's narrow but I reckon it's wide enough for the coach. Any questions?'

Yaniv stared at the two paths. They ran for three hundred metres before widening out onto an open shelf of land. The shelf was strewn with boulders and jagged rocks but it spelled safety.

'I'm not sure about this,' he said. 'No rope is ever going to hold that coach if it starts to slide. The path is like glass, half-frozen. Perhaps we should wait until my father gets back.'

'Damn your father, boy!' Tomas yelled. 'I'm fed up to my back teeth with your bloody father. He's not here. I'm making the decisions now.'

Yaniv stole a glance at Omar but the old soldier merely shrugged. He was used to obeying orders, no matter who they came from and regardless of whether or not he agreed with them.

It took just a few minutes to fit the landlines and two of the strongest troopers took up positions on the upper pathway. Yaniv felt a sudden pressure on his elbow and turned to see Sarah at his side. He explained what was happening. The girl frowned and shook her head.

'On that path? If the coach starts to slide it'll be over the edge before anyone can move.' She bent forward to stare into the chasm. 'Nobody is going to survive a fall down there. Hell, I can't even see the bottom. I just hope the stargazers are good at praying.'

They stood, watching, as the green coach began to creep along the path. Progress was slow, the coachman taking as much care as he could. Nobody spoke and Yaniv felt as if he had been holding his breath for ten minutes.

'What the hell is going on?'

Everyone spun around. Daniel Sharon was standing a few feet away, almost on the spot where he had been seen last. Trooper Hussain waited behind him. Yaniv felt a surge of joy but still cursed himself for lack of observation – like everyone else, he'd had eyes only for the drama that was unfolding before him.

'Who ordered this?' Sharon roared.

He glared at Tomas. The Corporal lowered his head – right or wrong it was too late to change anything now, the coach was already fifty metres into its journey.

'The stargazers?' Daniel demanded. 'Where are they?'

Tomas shrugged, a hopeless gesture of defeat.

'On the coach,' he said.

Daniel Sharon swore, leaped off the walkway and stormed across to the shamefaced Corporal. For a moment, Yaniv thought he would punch the man.

'On the coach? You damned fool - didn't you think to get them out first? If that coach goes over, they'll all go with it.'

The air was electric with tension as Daniel and Tomas stood face to face.

'Look!' Omar suddenly shouted.

He was pointing at the coach, now in the centre of the crossing. The white horses were struggling, pawing desperately at the ground to find a grip in the slush and snow.

'Left rein!' Sharon yelled. 'For God's sake, your left rein. Keep them close to the rock.'

It was good advice but it was already too late.

'I can't hold them,' screamed the coachman. 'We're going over.'

The heavily laden coach was sliding across the track, inching closer to the chasm's edge. The soldiers on the landlines pulled hard on their ropes, muscles bulging like knots of coiled wire. Then the coach took a sudden lurch to the right. Before he could let go of the rope around his shoulders, the soldier on the rear landline was whipped from his feet, landing on his stomach in the mud.

'Help!' he screamed, fingers clawing at the dirt and snow. 'Help me.'

He aquaplaned off the pathway onto the track below – and kept on going. Yaniv watched helplessly as the soldier's momentum took him across the track and over the edge. The sound of his scream echoed back off the sheer rock walls and then, mercifully, cut off abruptly.

Sarah turned her head into Yaniv's shoulder as the soldier on the other line dropped the rope and fell backwards in terror. The coach driver, seeing his danger, made one last effort to pull round the horses, then dived for safety. His body slammed into the rock wall with a dull thud that Yaniv fancied he could hear above the squealing of the terrified horses. The man staggered to his feet and raced to safety along the path.

The wheels of the coach spun round and round, the rear portion now hanging out over the chasm. One large trunk toppled from the roof, falling into the abyss and throwing out clothes and silks as it went. From inside the coach came terrified shouts.

'Get them out!' yelled Daniel Sharon. 'Quick,

while there's time.'

Without thinking, Yaniv darted forward. He covered the distance to the doomed carriage in seconds and yanked open the door. Reaching inside, he grabbed the ermine collar of the first man he saw and dragged him to his feet.

'Out, sir, quickly!'

He hurled the man across the path, the stargazer falling like an empty sack in the snow. A second stargazer was already halfway out and it needed only a hard push to get him to safety.

'Yanni,' Omar shouted. 'Look out, the coach is going. Get away while you can.'

There was still time to save the third man, Yaniv thought - just. He crawled into the coach and fell to his knees inside the door. The stargazer was lying against the outer window, a large package clutched in his arms, resigned to his fate.

'Quickly, sir, move!'

There was no response, the man staring at Yaniv with blank, unseeing eyes. Yaniv threw his arms around him and carried him to the door. Then he lost his footing, slipped and landed on top of the terrified man as, behind them, the coach finally toppled and fell.

For what seemed like hours, Yaniv and the

stargazer rolled like sagebrush on the edge of the chasm. Below them, the four white horses and the elegant green coach turned and spiralled as they plummeted into the depths. It was a vision that would stay with Yaniv forever and he could have wept at the waste of it all.

Daniel Sharon's strong arms suddenly enfolded Yaniv and the stargazer and pulled them back from the brink. The three men stood and stared into the abyss, the wind whipping at the stargazer's cloak. Yaniv shuddered at what might have been.

'Well done, Yanni,' his father whispered. 'Well done indeed.'

From far below came a roar like thunder as the coach hit the chasm floor.

'Sad,' breathed the stargazer, 'those beautiful horses, so sad.'

His voice was low and mellow and Yaniv realised it was the first time he had heard one of the Palace's precious astronomers talk. The man turned to face Yaniv.

'I thank you for my life, young man. Such bravery. Perhaps, one day, I will be able to repay you.'

Eyes twinkling, the stargazer walked with Daniel and Yaniv along the path to safety.

***

Daniel Sharon went into immediate discussion with the three stargazers. As they debated, dusk turned slowly into night, the planet Venus rising in the western heavens, never more beautiful, never brighter. Eventually Daniel approached the waiting troopers, his face serious.

'Right, this is what we are going to do. The supply wagons will never get across the track – they'll have to go back to the city. We need to unload them, get as much food and equipment as we can onto the horses. The wagons will have to make do with one horse each, the others we can use as pack animals.'

He glanced, briefly, at Sarah

'You'll come with us, girl. We will need your skills and your knowledge – you never know when we might require a cave or two. Do you have a companion, someone to help you, someone willing to share the dangers?'

Sarah nodded.

'My friend Anna, she's always saying how boring our job is.'

'I can't promise her much – or you. But boring it will never be.'

Corporal Tomas, eager to redeem himself, stepped forward.

'Should I go ahead, Sergeant – scout out a camp for the night?'

Daniel Sharon jabbed his thumb over his shoulder.

'It's already done, Corporal. What do you think Hussain and I were up to while you were trying to kill off the stargazers? A mile down the slope beyond this pass there's a village – a village with an inn. They are expecting us. Trooper Hussain, take Sarah and let the villagers know we are on our way. Get food ready, girl – I don't think a remote mountain inn will be capable of catering for our distinguished travellers.'

He stared at each of the soldiers, making sure that all of them understood his message.

'The stargazers want to go on. It won't be easy. They'll have to ride like the rest of us. But they are certain, their journey must continue.'

Yaniv glanced towards the shivering men of science and wondered just how they would make out over the next few days. Not easy, his father had said – for the stargazers it would be almost impossible. Daniel Sharon turned to his second-in-command.

'In the meantime, Corporal Tomas, you and I need to have a quiet chat.'

He strode away, Tomas following meekly in his wake.

'Start unloading those wagons,' Daniel threw back over his shoulder. 'Darkness is nearly on us and I want to be off the top of this damned mountain inside the next hour.'

'Come on, boy,' said Omar. 'You heard the man – we have work to do.'

He put his arm around Yaniv's shoulders and led him, carefully, back over the path towards the waiting supply wagons. It was the only praise he would ever receive from the old soldier but, to Yaniv, the gesture was worth a cabinet full of gold.

Chapter Four

They spent a warm but cramped night in the only room the inn could offer.

'Not much of a place,' said Omar. 'I can't imagine they get many travellers up here. We must be a godsend to them.'

They banked the fire high and lay around the walls. The stargazers no longer had the luxury of their coach but Sarah and Anna managed to create a little space for them by walling off part of the room with boxes.

'It's a poor way to journey on,' Sarah said, 'but it's their choice.'

Anna nodded enthusiastically, already overawed by her friend and the standing she held with people like Sergeant Sharon.

'We'll look after them,' she declared. 'Won't we, Sarah?'

The oldest of the stargazers, the last man rescued by Yaniv, looked up when he heard their words. He reached out to take Anna by the hand.

'Needs must, young lady. We intend to finish our quest, even if it means putting up with conditions very different from those we are used to.'

Yaniv could not find it in his heart to criticise the man, or his companions. They were used to the riches of the Palace, and the idea of days spent sitting on the backs of flea-bitten nags could not have come easily to them.

'Cheer up, sir,' he said. 'My father has sent Omar out to find a wagon for you.'

The stargazer studied him intently. 'Really? You think that likely in a remote village like this? If any of them had such a thing as a wagon they would surely keep it for themselves.'

Yaniv did not reply, knowing the man was probably right, but then the stargazer spoke again.

'Your father is the Sergeant, yes? A capable man, I think, good at his job. And you, too, are now a soldier. Your name is Yaniv. Mine is Caspar.'

It was the first time any of the stargazers had made real contact with him and Yaniv seized the chance to speak further.

'I don't mean to be rude, sir, but do you really need to carry on with your journey? Wouldn't it be easier just to turn around and head back to the city?'

He glanced across to where the other stargazers were arranging their bedding. They were old men, almost as old as Caspar. In their rich tunics, studded with rubies and emeralds, they seemed totally out of place in the shabby old inn. Caspar shook his head.

'We must all of us follow our star.'

'Do you mean Venus? Is that your star? I've been watching it and I've never seen it shine so brightly.'

'It is beautiful, is it not? We follow its arc. It leads, we come behind.'

'Leads to what, sir, leads to where?'

'None of us know,' said the stargazer. 'But its journey across the Heavens has been foretold. You know how we study the stars? This one is very special, we believe.'

Yaniv would have asked more but a sudden flurry of activity at the door brought all their heads around. Omar stumbled into the room, dusting fresh snow from his head and shoulders.

'Cold as a butcher's shop out there,' he declared.

He bent and spoke into the Sergeant's ear. A few moments later Sharon pulled himself to his feet and strode over to Caspar.

'No wagon, sir. But we have managed to buy three camels for you. They're not much use up here but once we get off this mountain they'll be far better than the pack horses.'

'It's years since I sat on the back of a camel,' Caspar said, grimly. 'But I am sure the experience will be, shall we say, exciting.' His green eyes twinkled as he went off to tell his companions the news.

'Get some sleep, Yaniv,' said Daniel. 'We leave early in the morning. Already we're behind time.'

On the other side of the room, Corporal Tomas lay wrapped in his blanket, silent as a shroud. Even so, Yaniv knew that the little man was awake and listening. Whatever had passed between him and Daniel Sharon remained a secret but Yaniv guessed it could not have been pleasant. He did not know the man well but even with his limited knowledge of the Corporal's character, it was clear that he would not take any reprimand easily.

* * *

They left at first light, the three stargazers perched on their unfamiliar mounts. Yaniv was used to seeing camels, beasts of burden plodding out of the desert with goods for the city, but the sight of three old men wobbling on the backs of these strange creatures made him laugh aloud.

49

'I'm glad you find it funny,' said Omar. 'It won't be easy getting those damned brutes down this mountain. No wonder the owners were happy to sell them. On the flat they're fine but up here? No use to anyone.'

Like a funeral procession, they inched forward over the litter of rocks, the steep downward incline dragging them forwards in their saddles. It was an exhausting and uncomfortable ride.

Towards mid-morning, Corporal Tomas came up the slope towards Yaniv and Omar at the rear of the column.

'At this rate,' Tomas said, 'we'll never get off this mountain. The Sergeant wants a new route.'

'Hold on,' Omar said. 'I'll conjure one up.'

'Oh yes, very funny,' Tomas sneered. 'Let's see how you like this – take two men, scout out to the left. You're looking for any trail or track that's easier than this one.'

He turned to Yaniv.

'You, come with me and Liman. We'll search off to the right.'

Yaniv felt a pang of unease. He had no wish to spend time with Tomas and Liman but he also knew that another way down the mountain had to be found.

For twenty minutes, they picked their way

over the rugged terrain. Their horses struggled and stumbled and, at last, they were forced to dismount. Tethering the animals to a large boulder, they continued the search on foot.

'Damn this!' cried Liman suddenly. 'There is no other route. It's just a waste of time.'

Yaniv felt inclined to agree with him. Then Corporal Tomas stopped dead in his tracks, pointing further out to the right.

'What's that, over there?'

They walked carefully towards what seemed to be a long black line across the snow. Only as they came closer did they see it was a crack in the ground.

'Goes down a long way,' said Liman, leaning forward to stare. 'It's a fault in the rock. Maybe it opened up after the last earthquake. Take a look.'

He stood back to let Yaniv gaze into the chasm.

Yaniv leaned forward. The split in the ground was narrow and dark. After the first few metres, he could see nothing.

'It's deep all right,' he said.

He felt a sudden hard push in the middle of his back and the next second he was falling, arms flailing as the rock face flashed past. His last memory was of Liman's grinning face, peering down at him. Then he felt a terrific blow on his back and everything went black.

***

From far away Yaniv thought he heard someone calling his name. The voice was faint and it was a nuisance. All he wanted was sleep and he turned on his side to block out the voice.

'No, Yaniv, stay still.'

It was a girl's voice and it came from somewhere above him. He opened his eyes.

'Sarah, is that you?'

He put up his hands to rub his eyes. Sarah's dark hair suddenly took shape, outlined against the sky at the top of the opening.

'Yaniv,' Sarah called again, 'you mustn't move. You're on a ledge – roll the wrong way and you'll fall to the bottom. You must stay still until I get help.'

'Be quick, Sarah,' Yaniv called, his head beginning to clear.

His throat felt dry and his back hurt. He did not know how long he had been unconscious but, clearly, he was still winded.

'You stay still, right?' Sarah shouted. 'I'll be back as soon as I can.'

Her head disappeared and Yaniv breathed out with relief. It was lonely in the darkness but at least help was on its way. Carefully, he checked himself for cuts or breaks, all the time conscious of the drop alongside him. Nothing seemed to be broken, even though his whole body throbbed like a decaying tooth.

For what seemed like hours, he lay in the darkness. Every so often, a shower of rocks tumbled down from the top of the chasm, sometimes hurtling onwards into the depths, sometimes scattering like pebbles across his body. As he lay, Yaniv thought about what had happened.

Liman had pushed him and Tomas had obviously engineered the whole trap. He would kill the pair of them when he got out. He did not understand their motive and he didn't really care. All he wanted was revenge.

At last, he heard the sound of hurried footsteps and voices calling. Then Sarah's head appeared once more on the skyline and this time she was accompanied by Daniel Sharon and Omar.

'Stay calm, Yanni,' Daniel shouted. 'We'll soon have you out of there.'

A length of rope snaked down and within seconds Omar was sliding down to perch beside him on the ledge.

'You were lucky,' the old soldier grunted. 'Look.'

He held out the blazing torch he carried in his left hand and let it drop into the void.

Flickering, it fell further and further into the darkness.

'Another foot to the right,' Omar said, 'and you'd have been down there with it.'

He slipped the end of the rope around Yaniv's waist and tugged at it.

'What is it about you and heights?' Omar laughed as Yaniv was lifted off the ledge, swinging precariously over the drop. 'Don't look down, boy - just close your eyes and pray.'

It was a painful haul up to the top, the rope biting into his flesh, but in two or three minutes he was out, standing gasping for breath in the strengthening wind.

'Thank you,' Yaniv mumbled once Omar had rejoined them. 'You saved my life.'

'Don't thank us,' said Daniel, 'thank Sarah. When Tomas and Liman came back alone she guessed there was something wrong.'

'They said you'd gone too close to the edge,' Sarah said, 'told everyone you'd fallen. I didn't believe a word of it so I followed your tracks and found the fault. You know the rest.'

Yaniv reached out to squeeze her hand. They did not speak; there was no need. Daniel put his arm around his son's shoulder and guided him to the horses.

'Can you ride?'

'I'll manage,' Yaniv replied. 'And when I get back I'll deal with Corporal bloody Tomas and his mate.'

Omar, helping him gingerly into the saddle, shook his head.

'You'll be lucky. They've gone, deserted. As soon as Sarah came into camp shouting that she'd found you, they knew the game was up. One minute they were there, the next they'd gone.'

Yaniv glanced at his father. Daniel patted his son on the knee, staring up into his face.

'You were right, Yanni, Tomas was no good. He and Liman took some of our supplies when they went. Even so, we're better off without them.'

They rode slowly, each pace sending waves of pain up Yaniv's spine. Camp had been set up in the lee of three large boulders. Long tarpaulins linked the three outcrops and winking yellow fires gleamed out a welcome.

They had laid out his blanket and Anna had prepared a dish of hot pottage. While he ate, Sarah heated two large stones and covered them in cloth. She laid the stones at Yaniv's side and he felt the warmth oozing into his battered body. He was suddenly very sleepy.

'Shock,' Sarah announced, 'nothing to worry about. You'll be a lot better in the morning.'

'No guard duty for you tonight, Yanni,' said Omar. 'Orders from me, Corporal Omar.'

Yaniv stared at him. Omar simply shrugged.

'Your father made me an offer I couldn't refuse. He told me I could take the promotion or start walking back to the city. That's a long way for an old man like me.'

Eyes closed and relaxed, Yaniv wondered briefly where the two deserters would go. Somehow, he knew they had not gone forever and he would be seeing them again, perhaps sooner than he wanted.

Chapter Five

Next morning Sarah inspected his bruised back and neck, reassuring him that nothing was broken.

'You'll heal – you have a soldier's head. Think you'll be able to ride today?'

The stargazers were concerned, one of them reaching into his pack and pulling out a bottle of milky liquid.

'Rub this into his back,' he told Sarah. 'It won't heal him but it will make the pain more bearable.'

Sarah took the bottle and sniffed it. She wrinkled her nose.

'It smells like sick.'

'True,' Caspar said, 'but it is good. Do as my friend Melchior suggests. He is a healer of note. Do it now before the day's ride begins.'

The liquid burned like fire, but after Sarah had spent five minutes working it into every pore on his back the ache seemed surprisingly better.

'You smell like a latrine,' Sarah told him as they rode off. 'Remind me to stay upwind of you today.'

Soon it began to snow again. Before five minutes had passed, the wind was whipping across the hills and they could barely see a horse's length in front of them.

'Whiteout,' Omar hissed. 'We need to find shelter soon or we'll lose direction and end up going round in circles till we drop.'

Once again it was Sarah who saved them, riding at full gallop up the column to show Sergeant Sharon three old drovers' huts that her people often used. They were broken down, without windows or doors, but they gave some shelter. They spent a boring afternoon and night, trying to keep warm. Next morning it had stopped snowing but it was still bitterly cold.

It was a long, hard ride down the western flank of the mountain and it was an hour to sunset before they finally came off the slopes. The snow had disappeared and soon the jumble of rock and debris gave way to coarse scrub and sand.

'We stop here,' Omar called. 'Come on, lads, the sooner we set up camp, the sooner we can all be warm and well fed.'

Another massage with Melchior's lotion, some more of Sarah's hot stones, and Yaniv felt relaxed again. He was just dropping off to sleep when Caspar suddenly appeared at his side.

'Stay in your blankets, Yaniv. I only came to see how Melchior's lotion was working.'

'It's been wonderful. It seems you stargazers do more than just stare at the Heavens.'

Caspar settled himself on the sand and lay back.

'Oh, we're interested in all sorts of things.'

They gazed up at the night sky, their eyes inevitably drawn to the pulsing speck of light that hung above them.

'That is Venus, isn't it?' Yaniv asked.

'Yes – but I've never seen it so bright. And it's moving fast, faster than we ever thought possible. That's why we have to journey so quickly, to keep pace with it.'

'What's at the end of it, the end of your quest?' Yaniv asked.

Caspar's eyes burned with hunger and excitement.

'We're not sure. There are so many prophesies concerning that star. One says that it will only come to rest over the birthplace of a King. Maybe that's true but we don't know – it's why we follow the star, to find out the truth.'

'But there might be nothing there.'

'If that is how it must be. Everything is

mapped out and planned, everything. So the coach going over the cliff, the horses, the soldier who fell – their time had come. Even you being pushed into the chasm, that had been written long ago. You survived because it was not your time. We cannot change our destiny so there is no reason to worry.'

He stretched and then rose to his feet.

'If there is nothing at the end of our journey it does not matter. The journey, the search, will have been worth the effort.'

Yaniv pondered on his words. It was a strange philosophy, one Yaniv could not share. Surely we have some control over our destiny, he thought, otherwise what was the point of life? He lay, staring at the bright glow of Venus as it pulsed like a beating heart above him. He hoped there would be something for the stargazers at the end of the journey. Even a new King.

* * *

The attack came at first light. Yaniv heard the shouts and threw back his blanket. As he was crawling to his feet, an arrow whipped past his face and embedded itself in one of the saddlebags.

'Ambush!' someone shouted. 'We're under attack!'

Yaniv dived for his sword, heart hammering

in his chest. He had already seen danger, several times, but this was different. This time he faced lethal weapons in the hands of experienced warriors.

'Form a square!'

He heard his father's command and ran to his side.

'Down on the ground, gentlemen,' Daniel said to the stargazers.

Safe within the square of soldiers, the stargazers did as they were told. Yaniv stood, shield and sword in hand, squinting into the semi-darkness.

'There!'

He followed Omar's outstretched arm. Horsemen were galloping around the camp, shrieking and waving spears in the air.

'That one,' said Daniel Sharon, pointing at the leading rider.

Trooper Hussain pulled back his bowstring and let the arrow fly. The missile smashed into the rider's chest with a thud that echoed above the roar of battle. The man screamed, toppled from his horse and lay, motionless, in the dust.

The next second Yaniv was fighting for his life. A huge warrior, face streaked with black, stood in front of him, his sword already beginning to sweep down at his head. Yaniv parried the blow but the shock threw him to the ground. He tried to claw his way to his feet.

A blow on his helmet smashed him sideways and his sword slipped from his grasp. The warrior raised his weapon for the final strike.

It never came. The man suddenly staggered, gazing in amazement at the sword blade that had cut through his protective leather jerkin and was now sticking out six inches from his chest. Daniel Sharon kicked the man to his knees and pulled out his sword.

'Always watch the other man, Yanni,' Daniel said, 'not the one you're attacking – a lesson he should have learned.'

The next five minutes passed in a haze. Yaniv struck at fleeting shapes but, later, he had no recollection of hitting anyone. The noise was intense, the clash of sword on sword mixed with the cries of wounded men and the neighs of terrified horses. Then, as quickly as it had begun, the attack was over.

Suddenly there were no charging men, no war cries, just silence. Yaniv stood, panting, staring around. Here and there bodies lay huddled on the ground and the occasional riderless horse stood cropping at the desert tundra.

'Count the dead,' Daniel Sharon ordered.

Yaniv felt empty. His first action was over and he had survived. He slid his sword into its scabbard and pushed his helmet to the back of his head.

'Four of theirs,' Omar reported. 'Three dead, one wounded and likely to die pretty soon. Just two of ours, Trooper Hussain and one of the Palace servant girls.'

Yaniv felt his stomach contract. Please God, he whispered, let it not be Sarah.

'The young girl, Anna, a sword thrust in the belly,' Omar continued. 'And Hussain took an arrow through the throat.'

Despite himself, Yaniv felt relief flooding his body. Sarah was safe. Poor Anna, he thought, all she ever wanted was to be like her hero, Sarah. And Hussain, so big and friendly. He was the second of their soldiers to die. With Tomas and Liman as having deserted, there were only eight troopers left now.

'Interrogate the wounded man,' Daniel said. 'Bandits don't normally attack Palace Guards – I want to know what this was about.'

Omar saluted and strode away. A few minutes later muffled screams began to roll from the far side of the camp. Yaniv shut his mind to them, knowing but not wanting to know what was happening. It was not long before Omar reappeared.

'He didn't want to talk – at first. In the end he decided to unburden his soul, which was probably as well, seeing he had so little time left.' He glanced at Yaniv, then back to the Sergeant. 'They weren't bandits, sir, just men from the next village. It seems that a couple of riders passed through last night, told them we were coming to burn the village, to destroy their crops and animals. They decided to get their retaliation in first.'

'Tomas and Liman,' Daniel roared. 'Dear God, let me catch up with them soon.'

Nobody spoke. Everyone felt the same.

'All right,' said the Sergeant at last. 'Let's bury the dead.'

* * *

For the next five days they rode across the desert, camping each night under skies so vast they seemed to go on forever. The days were hot, the burning sun turning the desert into a shimmering cauldron. The moment the sun slipped below the horizon, however, it was as if an iron fist had seized the land. No matter how much they banked up their fires, the cold seemed to eat into their bones.

'This must be the only country in the world,' Sarah said, bitterly, 'where you can get sunburn in the day and frostbite at night.'

Yaniv gently laid an extra blanket across her shoulders. She was, he knew, mourning the loss of Anna, blaming herself for the girl's death. He sought desperately for a way to bring her out of herself, to lift her gloom and guilt.

'The star is really bright tonight,' he said at last. 'The stargazers say it's Venus. I suppose they should know.'

Sarah was dismissive. 'Venus? I doubt it. I've seen the thing hundreds of times and it's never been as bright as this. Planets don't twinkle the way this one does – and sometimes, in the early morning, it seems to have a tail stretching out behind it.'

'So if not Venus, then what is it?'

Sarah lay back on the cold sand and adjusted her blankets.

'I don't know. Ask your friend Caspar if you're that interested.'

Caspar did not want to commit himself when Yaniv approached him next morning. The old man was loping along on his camel, eyes closed, half-asleep, swaying to the movement of his mount.

'It might be Venus. It might be a new star. I must have spent hours simply staring at it, day and night, and I'm still none the wiser.'

'In the day?' Yaniv said, puzzled. 'How can

you see stars in broad daylight?'

'Stars don't disappear when day comes like the ignorant and superstitious believe. They are still there, just difficult to see because of the sunlight. But we have a way.'

He reached into his saddlebag and pulled out a small square of glass, hardly bigger than his hand. It was blackened and as dark as jet. He passed it to Yaniv.

'Hold it up,' Caspar commanded. 'Look through it.'

To Yaniv's amazement, the sky was suddenly full of bright blazing stars. The one star, Venus or whatever it was, seemed almost as bright as the sun.

'It beckons us westwards,' said the stargazer. 'It's never still, not even for a moment, so perhaps it is a comet or a brand new star.'

Yaniv could have spent hours gazing through Caspar's glass but he saw the old man's outstretched hand and reluctantly passed it back. He should have returned to his place in the column but everything seemed quiet and there was so much he wanted to know.

'Will you tell me about the stars?' he said, the words gushing out in a torrent. 'And the planets. I want to learn.'

Caspar reached out to squeeze his arm. His

eyes were warm.

'An interested soldier – you are a rarity, boy. What is it you want to know?'

'Everything. Why the stars are up there, what they're made from. Can we ever reach out to touch them? I want to know everything.'

'Well,' smiled Caspar, 'that should keep us occupied for a few miles. All right, Yanni, listen.'

The old man began to speak as, together, they rode on across the desert.

Chapter Six

Later that day the atmosphere grew more temperate and clumps of grass began to litter the plain. As darkness settled like a blanket over the land, they saw the tall outline of palm trees against the sky.

'Oasis,' Omar declared. 'Your father is a miracle worker, Yanni. He's had this place in mind for the past three days. And we've hit it right on time.'

They set up camp, tethering the horses beneath the trees. There were no other travellers at the oasis that night and the troopers lay in comfort, like visiting kings. The night was warm, very different from the icy coldness of the desert.

'How much further, do you think?' Yaniv asked. He was sitting, staring at the flames of the campfire. He felt warm and comfortable.

Sarah smiled at him, sadly. 'I don't suppose anyone knows, not even the stargazers.'

She passed him a beaker of warm wine. The mixture was heavy and aromatic and Yaniv felt his head spin as he sipped at the drink.

'According to Caspar they just follow where the star leads,' he said.

'Then we could be travelling forever,' Sarah sighed. 'I've heard the legend, Yanni. It's meant to show the birthplace of a King. But that's only a story, nobody knows where or when it will stop moving.'

They lapsed into silence as Yaniv reached out to take her hand. For the first time since Anna's death, she did not pull away. Perhaps, he thought, she was starting to come to terms with the loss of her friend. At least he hoped so.

* * *

The horsemen appeared at dawn. The sentry saw them first, dark figures against the skyline, and called the alarm. When the lead rider appeared at the edge of the oasis, Daniel Sharon and his men were waiting.

'Fifty at least,' Omar whispered. 'We'll be lucky to get out of this with our skins intact. We're outnumbered five to one.'

Daniel Sharon pursed his lips and slowly shook his head.

'I don't think they're here to fight. If they were, we'd be food for the vultures by now. No, I think they just want to talk.'

The horsemen wheeled across in front of them. They were dressed in the distinctive blue and yellow livery of King Herod and every one carried a long lance. Some held pennants, small triangular flags, on the tips of their lances. Their commander came to a halt a metre in front of Daniel Sharon.

'Greetings from King Herod, lord and ruler of this land – which includes this oasis.'

He swung his leg over the neck of his horse and dropped lightly to the ground. Daniel eyed him carefully, ignoring the threat in his words.

'King Herod wasn't here last night. Otherwise I would have asked his permission to make camp.'

Yaniv tightened his grip on the handle of his sword, watching the two men measuring themselves and their positions. Finally, the newcomer dropped his gaze and shrugged.

'We won't quibble over a little water. I am Colonel Barak of the King's Bodyguard.'

He glanced at Daniel's small troop, nodding his approval.

'A well-turned-out unit, Sergeant – despite many days on the road.'

Beneath his words of flattery, Barak's tone was icy and contemptuous. Yaniv doubted whether he was really a Colonel but Colonel sounded better than Captain or Lieutenant – and certainly a lot more impressive than Sergeant.

'King Herod has ordered me to bring you to his Palace,' Barak continued. 'You have no objections?'

Daniel Sharon watched the man carefully. Finally, he turned to Omar.

'Stay here with the troop. I'll be back as soon as I have seen the King.'

Colonel Barak shook his head. 'The invitation is for all of you. The King insists that you all enjoy his hospitality.' His eyes swung round to the stargazers. 'The astrologers, in particular.'

They broke camp quickly as Herod's men sat on their horses and watched.

'Invitation, my foot,' Sarah stormed, pulling hard on the packing ropes of her favourite horse. 'He might call it an invitation. We're prisoners in everything but name.'

'If we resist,' said Yaniv, 'we'll all be dead in minutes.'

Sarah nodded. 'I know but I hate people like that telling me what I'm going to do.'

Yaniv said nothing but was secretly glad that Colonel Barak had at least taken her mind off poor Anna.

'They must have known we were coming,' said Omar as they rode. 'They'd never have come all this way on the off-chance of

71

meeting up with us.'

'How much further to Herod's Palace?' Yaniv asked.

'A long way yet. It's about ten miles south of Bethlehem. I've only seen it from the outside but they say it's the height of luxury – which is what you'd expect from someone like Herod. There's no way we're going to make it today. We'll have to camp somewhere – I expect Colonel Barak will have somewhere in mind.'

He did. Just before dark they pulled off the track into another oasis. There were a few other travellers grouped around the well, but seeing the long line of soldiers approaching they quickly withdrew to the far side of the oasis.

As always, Yaniv welcomed the glow of the night fires even though, this time, Herod's men were sitting with them as well.

'How far have you come?' one of them asked.

From the beginning, the two groups of soldiers had mixed well. It was often so. With soldiers, comradeship crossed the barriers of race and political alliances. Omar glanced at the man.

'A long way, my friend, from beyond the Yemen. God knows how many miles we've covered. The trip over the mountains was damned near impossible.'

The soldier nodded, clearly impressed.

'I was up there once. Never again, I say. Thank God King Herod is only interested in Judea and the land around Lake Galilee.'

'He sent you to look for us?'

'So it seems,' the soldier said. 'We're just like you, obeying orders. Barak knows our purpose – we just do as we're told.'

The man seemed sincere enough and Yaniv was inclined to believe him. With food eaten, they settled down to sleep, the two bands of soldiers lying silently together.

* * *

When Roman soldiers appeared at noon the next day, they were still a dozen miles from Herod's Palace. Yaniv had never seen Romans before. The cohort came marching over the crest of a small hill, walking with an easy swagger that came only with experience.

'They're not Romans,' Yaniv hissed.

Omar grinned at him. 'They're not Legionaries, I agree. But they are Roman soldiers – Auxiliaries. Legionaries come from Rome, Auxiliaries from all the countries their Empire has conquered. There are no Legionaries in Palestine, apart from the odd officer and Centurion.'

They may not have been Legionaries, Yaniv thought, but the cohort was certainly well drilled. He watched as they came to a halt, swords drawn but pointing downwards to the sand. The Centurion moved forward to speak to Colonel Barak and Daniel Sharon.

'Foot soldiers,' Yaniv said, 'in this heat?'

He stared at the men's red tunics, their breastplates and plumed helmets. They were sweating but all of them breathed easily. Unlike the men of Herod's Bodyguard, none of them smiled or waved a greeting to their fellow soldiers. These men were hard, unflinching, part of a war machine that had conquered almost the whole world. They were an unbeatable force and they knew it.

'The greatest soldiers in the world,' Omar snarled. 'The bastards!'

'All good men,' said the Centurion, overhearing Omar's comment and breaking away from Barak and Daniel. 'All ready to die for the Empire.'

He studied Omar and Yaniv, weighing them up, then nodded, happy with what he had seen.

'Perhaps you should consider joining us. We need good fighting men.'

Omar turned away with a sneer and Yaniv shook his head.

'Not yet, sir, I still have much to learn. Perhaps in time.'

The Centurion nodded and moved back to his men.

'My name is Marcus,' he called, 'should you change your mind. You can always find me in the barracks at Jerusalem.'

The Roman soldiers came to attention, then moved away. Marcus stared at Yaniv as they went past but made no comment. Nobody was sorry to see them go.

'Herod thinks he rules this country,' said Omar, 'but he does it on sufferance. The Romans are the real rulers of Palestine.'

With a shrill bark, Daniel Sharon called his troop together.

'There's chaos in Bethlehem. The Romans have ordered some sort of census and people are coming in from all parts of the country.'

'Surely that doesn't concern us, sir,' said Omar. 'We're heading for Herod's Palace, aren't we?'

Daniel Sharon nodded. 'At the moment, yes. But who knows what lies in the future? According to Marcus there is no accommodation to be found anywhere in the city.'

When the tall towers of King Herod's Palace finally took shape on the horizon it looked, as

Omar had said, magnificent. It stood on a slight incline, no other buildings within fifty metres of its walls. Built of heavy lime blocks, it was painted a delicate shade of pink. Brightly coloured flags fluttered gaily on the top of every tower.

The pealing of a single trumpet announced their arrival. They rode across a wooden bridge, hooves clattering like cymbals in the afternoon heat, and found themselves in a sheltered courtyard. An elegant chamberlain met them, robes as bright as those of the stargazers and with a yellow turban on his head.

'Welcome, welcome,' he cried. 'Come, your horses will be cared for. There are baths and clean clothes for you all. Your uniforms will be washed, ready for the morning.'

He stared at the dishevelled troop, nose wrinkling in disdain.

'Our weapons?' asked Sharon.

'Take them with you to your quarters - though you will not need them. You are not prisoners, you are honoured guests, and we know you soldiers feel naked without your swords.'

He led the way inside. Long, cool arcades of marble stretched before them with guards positioned at every corner. Yaniv felt he had walked for miles before the chamberlain flung open a heavy wooden door and ushered them into a spacious chamber. The walls were hung with tapestries and the rich aroma of incense filled the air.

'Make yourselves comfortable,' said the chamberlain. 'Our home is your home for as long as you choose. Baths and clean clothes are in the anteroom. Girls, if you want them, can be called in a moment. The King expects you in two hours – I will collect you.'

Then he was gone, leaving them to gawp at the splendour of the room. Omar threw off his tunic.

'Well, boys, I intend to enjoy this while I can. It's time for a bath.'

He glanced at Sarah.

'Sorry, girl – there must be a room for you somewhere.'

There was. She found a small antechamber and pulled the door shut firmly behind her.

'Stay out there,' she called. 'I'll kill the first man to set foot in here.'

Servants ushered the stargazers into another small chamber. An hour later, clean for the first time in weeks, everyone lay along the benches set around the room, Sarah with her hair wrapped in a white towel. Carefully, she sniffed at an orange on the table and began to peel it.

'It doesn't feel like we're prisoners,' she said. 'Perhaps Herod is genuine after all.'

'Take it for what it is, girl,' Omar sniffed, 'but don't believe any of it.'

The chamberlain arrived at the appointed hour, accompanied by a freshly uniformed Colonel Barak. The Colonel smiled at Daniel Sharon.

'Like toy soldiers,' he said.

'King Herod is ready,' the chamberlain announced as he led the way down the corridor. 'You look much more respectable now, Sergeant.'

Omar grunted and whispered in Yaniv's ear. 'He should try riding across the desert and mountains for a few weeks. Then we'll see how respectable he looks.'

Yaniv wished he had brought his sword and dagger with him. 'You won't need them,' the chamberlain had said but Herod's reputation for treachery did not fill him with confidence. They came to a halt before a double door. The chamberlain rapped loudly on the oak panelling.

'Come,' cried a voice from inside the room.

Colonel Barak pushed open the doors and they were ushered into the presence of King Herod.

Chapter Seven

At first glance, Herod the Great was not an imposing figure. Slight in build, with a long curling beard, he sat on a dais at the far end of the room. His fingers, resting on the arms of his ornate throne, twitched continually and Yaniv remembered what people said - the King suffered from deep depressions and moments of ferocious anger.

'Sit,' Herod commanded, 'take wine. I wish to speak with you, Sergeant, and the stargazers.'

His voice was surprisingly light, hardly what Yaniv expected from a man supposedly consumed by ambition and greed. Yaniv sat alongside Omar on the carpet and accepted the cup of wine that was thrust at him.

'Worth a year's wages,' said Omar, studying his golden beaker. 'I guess the wine is just as expensive.'

Yaniv had ears only for the conversation that was taking place at the front of the room.

'You have come a long way?' Herod asked.

'Yes, sire,' Daniel answered, 'a long, hard journey.'

'Guided by a star, I believe?'

Herod's voice had become suddenly sharp and his gaze swept from Daniel to the stargazers. They nodded agreement – there was no point in denial.

'We follow a star, as you say,' Caspar commented. 'The brightest one in the Heavens.'

'It leads us onwards,' said Melchior.

'You must have seen it,' urged Balthazar, the youngest of the three men. 'It is as bright as the sun.'

Balthazar rarely spoke, seeming to be always lost in his own thoughts and dreams. Now he was animated, his tongue loosened by the wine. Caspar reached out and laid a restraining hand on his arm. King Herod, however, was not to be denied.

'My scribes and magi have also studied this star. They have told me of the legend.'

'What legend?' said Caspar.

Herod snorted, waving his arm in the air in a gesture of dismissal.

'Do not treat me like a fool, stargazer. We both know the story. The star, they say, will show the birthplace of a King, an all-powerful King.'

81

'So they say,' shrugged Caspar, 'but there is no proof. That is one of the reasons we follow the star, to see what is at the end of its track.'

Herod stood suddenly and clapped his hands. Instantly, the doors at the side of the room were flung open and servants, carrying huge platters of food, swept in.

'We will talk as we eat,' Herod said. 'There is much to talk about.'

Food and drink kept coming all evening. Yaniv felt his head swimming with the effect of the rich spices and alcohol. Omar raised a warning finger.

'Take care, Yanni. Herod is a madman who killed his own family to seize power. He wouldn't hesitate to do the same to us if it suited him.'

Tonight, though, Herod's purposes were different. Tonight he wanted information.

'There is a theory,' he said, lying back on the cushions, his hookah pipe bubbling, 'a theory that the King will be born in Bethlehem, here in Judea.'

A momentary spasm of anger flashed across his mottled face. There was fear as well as fury in the expression. He was King of Judea; another ruler born in the region could only spell danger.

'It is possible,' said Caspar, 'depending on

where the star stops on its journey.'

'It has grown much brighter of late,' added Melchior. 'The further west we go, the more brightly it has shone.'

Herod pushed away his pipe and lurched to his feet. Everyone immediately stopped eating and talking.

'The star is still moving?'

'Still moving,' said Balthazar, 'and still shining brightly.'

Colonel Barak spoke suddenly. Herod swung around to face him.

'This new King,' Barak said. 'He will be King of what?'

'We do not know,' shrugged Caspar. 'He may be a successor to Lord Herod or he might simply be the ruler of a church. He may even be the leader of a gang of beggars. The term "King" can cover many possibilities. That's if the legend is true.'

Herod was pacing the floor and biting furiously at his knuckles. At last, he spun around to stare at the stargazers.

'Whatever he is, if this new King is born here, I need to see him. I must pay my respects - it is the least I can do as King of Judea.'

His voice was oily and soaked in sincerity. The stargazers bowed to him.

'Promise me one thing. If you find this new

King, will you return and tell me where he is? Then I can go and pay him homage.'

The stargazers rose to their feet, clearly impressed. Caspar grasped Herod's outstretched hand.

'Of course, my Lord. You have our word.'

* * *

Later that night, Daniel Sharon led his men back to their quarters. Sarah, who had not been invited to the banquet, was waiting to hear what had been discussed. As Yaniv reported, she shook her head in disbelief.

'You can't trust him. Herod is one of the most treacherous men in the world. All he's concerned about is his own power. He only wants to find this new King in order to kill him.'

'I agree,' said Yaniv, 'but it's not me who makes the decisions. The stargazers believe him. I suppose they're used to luxury like this and after the discomforts of the journey, they've been taken in by the pampering. They think he's genuine.'

As the others drifted off to sleep, Yaniv and Sarah sat and talked. Finally, a shouted rebuke from one of the troopers sent them scurrying outside. The star was still shining brightly, to the north of them now. Brighter than the new moon, it pulsed and throbbed in the sky.

'Do you think it really does show the birthplace of a new King?' Sarah asked. 'And if it does, what does that mean for Herod?'

Yaniv took her arm.

'Let's walk for a while.'

They strolled along the raised walkway around the Palace walls. Suddenly, Yaniv stopped and pointed.

'Is it just me or has the star stopped moving?'

Sarah followed his gaze.

'Perhaps. It's difficult to tell with just the naked eye. We need Caspar's glass.'

They stood and lined up the star against one of the flagpoles. For over a minute, they stared. The star certainly seemed to have stopped its transit.

'Over Bethlehem, you think?'

Bethlehem lay a dozen miles away, too far for the lights of the city to glow in the sky. If the legend was correct, that was where the new King was meant to be born.

'Perhaps Herod was right to be scared,' said Yaniv.

Sarah's head came up and she held her finger to her lips.

'Voices,' she said. 'Down there.'

She pointed to the terrace below. Yaniv edged to the parapet, and then stiffened in alarm. He swung round, ashen-faced.

'You'll never believe it,' he whispered. 'Take a look.'

Sarah inched up beside him. She gasped.

'Tomas and Liman,' she said, hoarsely. 'In Herod's livery, too.'

It made sense. The two deserters would have had to find employment, and Herod's Palace Guard was a logical choice. With their experience, Colonel Barak would have been mad to turn them down.

'What are they saying?' Sarah whispered.

Yaniv leaned over the parapet as far as he dared. The two men were seated on the edge of the terrace, deep in conversation. Unconcerned, they spoke easily and clearly.

'Well,' Liman said, 'it seems the attack by the villagers didn't delay them too long.'

'Did you expect it to?' snarled Tomas. 'It would need a lot more than a band of country yokels to take out Daniel Sharon. He's a damned good soldier.'

'So what now?'

'Barak says they leave at first light,' said Tomas, staring up at the burning star. 'All we have to do is follow them. The star seems to have stopped over Bethlehem so we stay a few miles back until they find the place where the baby lies.'

'And then we kill them?'

Tomas turned angrily on his comrade.

'No, you bloody fool. Herod wants to know where this child can be found. We leave the killing to him – the baby, the stargazers, Sharon and his troopers. We just report back to Colonel Barak, take our money and move on.'

He raised a goatskin flagon to his lips, drained it and let the empty bag fall to the ground.

'I'm for my bed,' he declared. 'It's yet another early start tomorrow.'

Tomas and Liman disappeared from view. Sarah gripped Yaniv's arm, her nails digging into his flesh.

'I told you Herod was up to no good. He's going to kill this new King. I don't care a fig for princes and kings but nobody has the right to murder a new-born baby.'

Yaniv's head was spinning. Herod had convinced the stargazers of his good intentions but he still planned to kill the one possible rival for his throne, a baby who was lying somewhere in Bethlehem. The whole thing was a mess and Yaniv knew there was only one hope – his father.

Daniel Sharon was asleep but woke quickly when Yaniv pressed his fingers into the flesh behind his ear – an old hunter's trick his father had shown him many years before.

'Come outside,' Yaniv hissed. 'We need to talk.'

They walked to the far wall of the Palace. Daniel listened carefully, saying nothing until his son had finished.

'You heard this, too?' he asked Sarah.

The girl nodded, clutching at Yaniv's arm for support. 'It's true, sir. Tomas and Liman are here. Tomorrow, when we leave, they intend following us. When they report to Colonel Barak, the killing will begin – of everyone who knows anything about the star.'

Daniel Sharon was silent, deep in thought. Suddenly he pulled himself erect.

'Find Omar, Yanni, bring him to me.'

Yaniv raced off and Daniel turned to Sarah.

'A difficult and dangerous time, girl. Our lives hang in the balance – does that worry you?'

'Not unduly. It's the baby I'm concerned about. We have to save him, sir.'

Daniel reached out and squeezed her shoulder. 'We will, girl, I promise you. We'll save him or die in the attempt.'

Chapter Eight

When they left the Palace next morning there was no sign of King Herod, but Colonel Barak and a detachment of cavalry was drawn up to see them go.

'Good luck, Sergeant,' Barak called. 'With luck we may meet again, very soon.'

'Only on the end of my lance,' Omar whispered.

The Colonel sat, rigid, as the troop rode past. He saluted the stargazers, then turned his horse and went back into the Palace.

They rode for several hours before dropping into a deep canyon where Daniel Sharon called a halt. Yaniv stood patiently as his father began to tell the stargazers about Herod's plans.

'Are you sure about this?' asked an agitated Caspar. 'King Herod was so interested in our quest - he cannot have meant harm to anyone.'

Balthazar and Melchior nodded in agreement.

'With respect, sir,' Daniel said, 'Herod isn't

the most trustworthy of men. My son, on the other hand, is totally honest.'

'Really?' Caspar's tone was hard and challenging. 'He is a young man with no experience of Kings and politics. Perhaps he misunderstood.'

'He didn't misunderstand anything, you stupid, blind old man!' Sarah, in no mood for argument, stood with her hands on her hips, staring Caspar down. Daniel Sharon stopped her with a wave of his hand.

'You will know the truth soon enough. Two of my men will wait here while we ride on. If there is a pursuit of any kind, they will bring us evidence and you will know Yaniv spoke the truth. Agreed?'

Caspar nodded, reluctantly. The troop and the stargazers remounted, leaving Yaniv and Omar in the gully. The old soldier shrugged.

'Some people you can't convince. Let's find ourselves a hiding place. We have an hour, I reckon.'

In fact, it was nearer two hours before they heard horses approaching.

'Two men,' said Omar, 'well mounted. Remember what we agreed – for the moment you stay hidden.'

They waited until the rattle of dislodged stones and rocks told them the riders were close. Then Omar stepped out onto the path. From his hiding place, Yaniv heard a sharp intake of breath and the whinny of startled horses.

'My God, Omar, you damned near frightened me to death.'

Corporal Tomas brought his horse under control but made no move to dismount. Omar grinned at him and pointed his finger.

'Following us, Tomas?' he asked, easily. 'The game's up. We know exactly what you're doing.'

'Doing? We're not doing anything.'

'You were overheard discussing it last night. And apart from anything else, those uniforms rather give you away.'

Tomas spread his arms wide. 'Omar, my friend, you have it all wrong.'

'Really? Let me put it this way – you're a pair of treacherous two-faced bastards and neither of you is going any further today. Go back to Herod and tell him that.'

'Damn you!' shouted Liman.

He urged his horse forward, sword raised, ready to run Omar through. Liman had hardly begun to move before he gave a loud grunt. He stared down in amazement, clawed briefly at the dagger that was now buried in his chest and then toppled from his horse. He was dead before he hit the ground. Tomas watched with surprising calmness.

'Poor Liman,' he said, 'always too headstrong for his own good.' He stared at Omar, a cold sneer pasted across his face. 'I see you haven't lost your skill with a throwing knife, old man. So who heard us talking last night? Does the Sergeant know?'

'It hardly matters. All you need to know is that you won't be reporting anything back to your new master.'

'Master?' Tomas spat. 'You mean that madman Herod. He is no master to me.'

He swung his leg over his saddle and dropped lightly to the ground. He glanced at the lifeless body of his friend and shook his head.

'The times I told him to go slowly but he never learned. Still, you've saved me the job of putting my knife between his ribs.'

'You would have killed him?'

'Oh yes, he was always dispensable. Herod and Barak have paid well but why split the money when you can have it all?'

Yaniv could contain himself no longer. Anger blazing, he leapt out onto the track to confront Tomas.

'You evil, treacherous rat,' he screamed, lunging forward with his sword.

Omar caught him, strong arms enveloping him, holding him tight.

'No, Yanni, not like this. We'll take him ...'

It was a mistake, the movement turning Omar's back to the Corporal, and Tomas reacted swiftly. Once, twice, the pommel of his sword smashed down on Omar's skull. As the old man collapsed into the dust, Tomas brought his sword up to Yaniv's throat.

'I wondered when the Sergeant's brat would appear. Well, boy, you've interfered with my plans once too often, you and your oaf of a friend.'

Yaniv glanced down at Omar's body, not knowing if he was alive or dead. The pool of blood beneath his head was not reassuring and Yaniv felt sorrow and hatred mesh together in his belly.

'What are you going to do?' he said, desperately playing for time.

Tomas edged forward. Yaniv felt the point of the sword prick into the skin below his chin. Strangely, he did not feel afraid.

'What am I going to do? What I was paid to do – follow your stargazers and, once I've found the place where this so-called King is waiting, report back to Colonel Barak. First, though, a little pleasure – on your knees, boy.'

For a moment, Yaniv thought of refusing

but he knew that every second was precious in finding a way out of this. And so, reluctantly, he kneeled in the dust.

'I would ask you to beg,' Tomas gloated, 'but we both know that would be a step too far for you. Let's just end it quickly.'

He swung the sword above his head. Yaniv closed his eyes and waited for the blow, praying it would be quick and painless.

'Open your eyes, boy,' Tomas snarled. 'I want you to look at what's coming.'

Yaniv squinted up at the man, wondering if he could throw himself at his legs and knock him to the ground. Tomas shook his head.

'Don't even think about it.'

There was a sudden hiss, like a snake's warning, and Tomas staggered forward. He half turned to search for his assailant and Yaniv saw the shaft of an arrow lodged in his back. A second arrow thumped into his side, throwing him against the rock wall. He clutched at the bolt, eyes already growing dim.

'No,' he gasped, 'not like this.'

A third arrow caught him full in the chest and Tomas slid silently to the ground. Yaniv, eyes only for the dead body, sensed another presence. A shadow fell across his face and he looked up into Sarah's piercing blue eyes.

'Good God, woman,' he managed to splutter.

'Where did you learn to shoot like that?'

Sarah slung her bow and knelt by his side.

'It's lucky for you I had a misspent youth. I learned to shoot before I could read and write.'

'Three arrows?' Yaniv said. 'Why three?'

Sarah shrugged.

'One to save you, one to put him out of his misery and the third' – she paused – 'the third for Anna.'

'Why are you here? Did my father send you?'

Sarah shook her head. 'I slipped away from the column. I guessed you'd be needing my help.'

She pulled Yaniv to his feet and they moved to where the old soldier still lay.

'He's alive, at least,' Sarah said, mopping at the congealed blood on the back of Omar's head. 'Get me some water, Yanni.'

Yaniv filled his helmet from a nearby stream, then gathered in the loose horses. He strapped the bodies of Liman and Tomas across their saddles and watched as Omar staggered to his feet.

'Are you all right to ride?' Yaniv asked.

'As long as you can do it, boy, so can I. I have an almighty headache but no permanent damage. Just help me to my horse.'

It was evening before they caught up with

the column. The troop had camped on a hill outside Bethlehem, picket fires glowing in the darkness. The town lay below them, a collection of small white houses with long streams of travellers heading from the gates.

Daniel Sharon cut the ropes holding Tomas and Liman, letting the two bodies fall to the ground.

'Misunderstood, stargazer?' Omar hissed at Caspar, pointing at the bodies. 'I think this proves that you were the one who misunderstood.'

Caspar bowed his head, then stepped forward to place his hand on Yaniv's shoulder.

'A thousand apologies, Yanni. You were right – Herod is not to be trusted.'

Yaniv shrugged. 'It doesn't matter. Tomas and Liman are dead. Herod will not receive any news from them.'

'Have you noticed? The star has stopped,' Caspar said. 'We have been watching for hours – it has come to rest over Bethlehem, as the legend predicted.'

Melchior took Omar aside to treat his wound while Yaniv and Sarah sat before the fire.

'It is time to see if there really is anyone or anything of note beneath the star,' said Caspar. 'We have been travelling a long time now –

there has to have been a purpose to it all.'

Yaniv noticed the uncertainty in his voice. For himself, he felt only a deep thrill. The quest was nearly over. Now it was time to find out the truth.

Chapter Nine

At midnight they broke camp and moved down the hill towards Bethlehem. With the star impaled above their heads, it was almost as bright as day and the stargazers led them through the gates, into the town. It was a poor enough place - narrow streets, houses that jutted out at awkward angles. Yet the stargazers seemed to know where they were going.

Despite the late hour, the place was crowded. Men and women strode along the streets, others, muffled and caped, lay or sat in the doorways, trying to snatch a few hours' rest. Yaniv remembered Marcus's words - no empty inns or lodging houses anywhere.

Finally, with the star directly over their heads, they came to a halt in front of a large inn. People were pushing in and out of the doors and the noise through the open windows told them that wine was still being served.

'This must be the place,' said Caspar.

The stargazers dismounted and Caspar

passed small packages to his friends. As the troopers stood alongside their horses, Caspar, Melchior and Balthazar went into the inn.

For ten minutes they waited, Yaniv more anxious than he cared to admit. He looked at Sarah and shrugged. The girl bit at her nails and wandered idly to the corner of the building, where she stood, staring into the adjoining alley. More minutes passed. Finally, the inn door swung open and the stargazers came out. Their faces were clouded with disappointment.

'No King, no new-born baby,' Caspar said. 'It's not the place.'

'But all our calculations told us it was here,' retorted Balthazar.

Melchior nodded. 'And the star, it led us here.'

He pointed at the Heavens. It was probably imagination, Yaniv thought, but as he looked up he was sure the star had gone suddenly dimmer, almost as if it knew its job had been completed. Everyone stared, then dropped their eyes to the ground. Sarah's voice suddenly cut through the night air.

'You've been looking in the wrong place,' she said, pointing to the alleyway at the side of the inn. 'Remember what Marcus the Centurion said - no room at any of the inns during the census. Follow me.'

She stalked away down the alley, followed by the troopers and the stargazers. They came to a halt in front of a small lean-to, hollowed out of the rock and finished with pieces of rough wood to make a barn or cattle shed.

'In here?' Caspar said. 'We're going in here?'

'We are if you want to find your King,' Sarah smiled.

They filed inside. Against the far wall a young girl sat, her feet covered in straw and a thin shawl draped around her shoulders. A tall man, heavily bearded, stood alongside her.

'These are the travellers you meant?' he asked.

Sarah nodded and turned to explain.

'While you were all waiting, I slipped down here. This is Joseph and this is Mary and there is the King you have been searching for.'

She pointed to a crude wooden manger, filled with straw. A baby, no more than a few days old, was lying peacefully in the crib. The child gazed happily around.

'A strange place for a King to be born,' said Daniel Sharon.

Mary smiled up at him.

'The innkeeper let us stay here when he saw my time was near. There was nowhere else.'

'And the baby,' said Caspar, 'he was born here?'

'Here in the stable, God's son born in a stable. He is to be the King of all humankind, not just Judea or Palestine. He is our Messiah.'

The three stargazers filed forward, knowing instinctively that this was right and that this was the end of their quest. Caspar knelt before the girl.

'We have gifts - gold and frankincense and myrrh, gifts for a King.'

The soldiers followed, each of them looking silently at the child. When it was his turn, Yaniv held out his finger. The baby took it in his hand and grinned up at him.

'Wind,' said Omar, smiling at Yaniv.

They stood in the stable for what seemed like hours. At last, Daniel Sharon broke the silence.

'I hate to say this, but there are people out there who do not relish the birth of your son.'

The child's father stood looking down into the manger.

'Like King Herod?' he said. 'To him this birth only provides a rival, someone to steal his throne. But this child is not that type of King.'

'Given the chance Herod would still kill your child. I think we have two, maybe three days, then Herod's soldiers will be here. We have to move quickly.'

Caspar clutched at his sleeve.

'You think you can keep them safe?'

'In battle? No chance. Colonel Barak, when he comes, will have a hundred men. But time is on our side – with Tomas and Liman gone he will have to wait longer for news. That gives us time to get them to safety, somewhere Herod and Barak would not think of looking.'

Silence fell across the stable.

'Egypt,' said Yaniv, suddenly.

Joseph and Sergeant Sharon stared at him.

Yaniv remembered Omar's description of Egypt, the land of milk and honey. And Omar had travelled there.

'It's within riding distance, a few weeks' journey, perhaps. Herod would not dream of looking there.'

They stood, considering Yaniv's words. Finally, Daniel Sharon strode across to the baby, then turned to face everyone. Yaniv could see the pride in his eyes.

'Yaniv is right. Egypt it must be.'

'It will be a long journey,' said Balthazar. 'Remember, we are old men who have already travelled hundreds of miles.'

'I wasn't thinking about all of us going,' said Daniel. 'We must split the party. Colonel Barak needs to see us heading north. It will be dangerous but without the child and his parents, he should leave us alone. Meanwhile, the child will be heading south under the guard of two of my men. If they leave tomorrow they will have a good start on Barak and will stand a fair chance of making it.'

He turned to the assembled soldiers.

'I can't order anyone to undertake this mission. It will be dangerous and it may take many months. I need two volunteers.'

Yaniv glanced at Sarah and smiled as the girl nodded her head.

'We'll do it,' Yaniv said. 'Sarah and me.'

* * *

They left the following day, Mary perched on the back of a donkey, Joseph squatting uncomfortably on a spare horse. Daniel Sharon stood alongside his son to bid him farewell.

'I will explain to your mother,' he said. 'She will understand.'

He and Yaniv laughed.

'Three months, I reckon,' said Daniel, 'maybe four. Keep a low profile. The whole purpose of your journey is to get the child and his parents to safety. Avoid Barak and anyone you're not sure about.'

He stood back, eyes misty with uncharacteristic emotion, then spun around to attend to his duties. Yaniv glanced back at Omar and Caspar, men who had become firm friends over the past few weeks.

Omar raised his hand in farewell. 'Come and see me on my farm,' he called.

'And come to the Palace to see me when you get back,' Caspar shouted.

Yaniv turned and followed Sarah along the road that led out of Bethlehem.

Chapter Ten

They had been travelling south for several long weeks and Herod's Palace and realm lay far behind them. As Sarah said, they were not safe yet but they were almost there.

Several times, they had seen soldiers on the skyline and once Yaniv swore he recognised Colonel Barak's tall figure at the head of one particular column. He pulled his party into the shelter of a large sand dune and when they looked again, sometime later, Barak had gone.

Apart from the occasional nomad or party of camel drovers, they had met almost no-one. And each night Yaniv would sit before their campfire and dandle the baby on his knee.

'Sometimes,' he told Sarah, 'he looks at me as if he knows everything, as if he is already a million years old.'

The girl playfully punched his arm.

'Wouldn't you, if you were the son of God?'

He had to agree with her. Son of God or not, there was certainly something special about this little boy.

At last, the sand dunes began to ease out and

the land became level and green. And then one morning the River Nile was there ahead of them and, on the banks, a collection of low white houses.

Joseph went off to find lodgings while Yaniv sat and played with the baby for the last time.

'You'll miss him,' Sarah said.

'I will. But, do you know, I have a feeling I will be seeing him again. I don't know where or when but I know we will meet again.'

That afternoon they took Mary and the child to the house that Joseph had found.

'Won't you stay for a few days?' Mary asked. 'You need a little rest before you start back.'

Yaniv shook his head. 'I have to get back to my unit. And besides, my mother will be worried sick until I return.'

They laughed. Herod and Barak could not scare him but his mother was a different matter. Sarah and Yaniv left the next morning. Mary and Joseph stood at the house door, waving goodbye.

'We will never forget you,' Mary called.

Yaniv turned his face to the north and whispered to himself, 'And I will never forget you.'

Sarah reached out for his hand and, side by side, they rode out of Egypt.

Gun Shy

Vidar, the army search dog, spent half his life sniffing out enemy weapons and bombs on the front line of the war in Afghanistan. His keen nose saved the lives of hundreds of soldiers, finding roadside bombs which could have killed British troops. But after two years of loyal service, Vidar became 'Gun Shy' – a term used to describe dogs who are frightened of loud noises. Whenever he heard bombs exploding or even the sound of helicopters flying above, he would curl up in the corner, shaking with fear.

His army days were numbered... and his future looked uncertain. Until Angie, an army medic who befriended him during her tour of Afghanistan, made it her duty to give him a safe haven at her Welsh home.

For more information about
Phil Carradice
and other **Accent Press** titles,
please visit:

www.accentpress.co.uk

110